MOON FLIGHT ATLAS

THE ASTRONAUTS

SPACE SURVIVAL

DAVID JEFFERIS

CRABTREE
PUBLISHING COMPANY
WWW.CRABTREEBOOKS.COM

INTRODUCTION

In the 1960s, the United States and **Soviet Union** were rivals in space.This competition was called the Space Race. At first, the Soviets led the way, but the U.S. caught up, and became the first to land on the Moon.

     The U.S. space agency **NASA** directed the Mercury space program, followed by the Gemini and **Apollo** programs. The aim was for astronauts to land on the Moon—and then return safely to Earth.

 Crabtree Publishing Company

www.crabtreebooks.com   1-800-387-7650

Copyright © **2019 CRABTREE PUBLISHING COMPANY**.

Written and produced for Crabtree Publishing by:
David Jefferis

Technical advisor:
Mat Irvine FBIS (Fellow of the British Interplanetary Society)

Editors:
Mat Irvine, Ellen Roger

Proofreader:
Melissa Boyce

Prepress Technicians:
Mat Irvine, Ken Wright

Print Coordinator:
Katherine Berti

Acknowledgements
We wish to thank all those people who have helped to create this publication and provided images.

Individuals:
Mat Irvine
David Jefferis
Rolf Klep
Davis Meltzer
Gavin Page/Design Shop

Organizations:
Fisher Pen Company
NASA
Smithsonian National Air and Space Museum
The Observer, London

The right of David Jefferis to be identified as the Author of this work has been asserted by him in accordance with the Copyrights, Designs and Patents Act 1988.

Printed in the U.S.A./042019/CG20190215

Library and Archives Canada Cataloguing in Publication

Jefferis, David, author
    The astronauts : space survival / David Jefferis.

(Moon flight atlas)
Includes index.
Issued in print and electronic formats.
ISBN 978-0-7787-5411-4 (hardcover).--
ISBN 978-0-7787-5420-6 (softcover).--
ISBN 978-1-4271-2215-5 (HTML)

    1. Life support systems (Space environment)--Juvenile literature. 2. Space flight--Physiological effect--Juvenile literature. 3. Astronauts Juvenile literature. 4. Space flight to the moon--History--Juvenile literature. 5. Moon--Exploration--History--Juvenile literature. 6. Moon--Maps--Juvenile literature. I. Title.

TL1500.J44 2019   j629.   C2018-905621-5
                                  C2018-905622-3

Library of Congress Cataloging-in-Publication Data

Names: Jefferis, David, author.
Title: The astronauts : space survival / David Jefferis.
Description: New York, New York : Crabtree Publishing Company, [2019] | Series: Moon flight atlas | Includes index.
Identifiers: LCCN 2018060555 (print) | LCCN 2019000503 (ebook) |
    ISBN 9781427122155 (Electronic) |
    ISBN 9780778754114 (hardcover : alk. paper) |
    ISBN 9780778754206 (pbk. : alk. paper)
Subjects: LCSH: Astronauts--United States--Juvenile literature. | Astronauts--Training--Juvenile literature. | Space flight to the moon--Juvenile literature. | Extravehicular space suits--Juvenile literature. | Astronautics--Miscellanea--Juvenile literature.
Classification: LCC TL793 (ebook) | LCC TL793 .J41955 2019 (print) | DDC 629.45/07--dc23
LC record available at https://lccn.loc.gov/2018060555

MOON FLIGHT ATLAS

CONTENTS

HIGH-FLYING PIONEERS

Even before the dawn of space flight, aircraft designers and pilots tried to break records for speed and height.

??? **Who was the first aviator to make really high flights?**

American aviator Wiley Post became famous in the 1930s for his extreme flights. Post broke many long-distance and height records, often while flying in a Lockheed Vega, a single-engined plane he named the *Winnie Mae*.

Lockheed Vega

For his high-altitude flights, Wiley designed a special suit (*right*). It was the ancestor of **pressure suits** worn by the pilots of jet and rocket planes, and the space suits later used by astronauts and cosmonauts.

➜ **This Wiley Post suit had a helmet made of aluminum. The circular faceplate could be opened like a ship's porthole.**

??? Were there realistic movies made about the Moon?

Among the best was *Destination Moon*, released in 1950. The poster (*left*) depicted the moonscape as a desert with steep mountains. Nobody knew what the landscape really looked like. In real life, the mountains of the Moon turned out to be gently rounded, rather than the jagged peaks seen here.

??? What rocket research planes made high flights?

Exploring the upper air was a big target for aviation in the 1950s, and rocket power was the only way to get there.

A series of experimental X-planes were built to be lifted to high altitude by a mother plane. The X-plane was then dropped, and its rocket motor was fired by the pilot to fly higher and faster.

When the X-plane's fuel was used, the pilot flew it as a glider down to Earth.

"If the mask is not tight, conscious time at 48,000 feet (14,630 m) cockpit altitude is approximately 15 seconds."
Warning about wearing oxygen masks safely, given to pilots of the Canadian CF-100D jet (right)

→ The Douglas Skyrocket rocket plane was launched in midair. On one such flight, a Skyrocket roared along at a record-breaking 1,291 miles per hour (2,078 kph).

INTO THE UNKNOWN

The first spacecraft was **Sputnik** 1, which circled Earth in 1957. But it was four more years before a human went into **orbit**.

??? What is an orbit?

This is where a spacecraft circles Earth, having reached a speed of around 17,500 miles per hour (28,164 kph). A lower speed results in a spacecraft falling back to Earth before reaching orbit—a suborbital path. Developing rockets powerful enough to send a spacecraft into orbit was a massive job, which became possible only in the late 1950s.

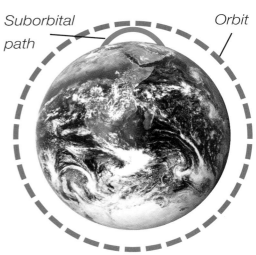

Suborbital path *Orbit*

↑ An orbit (*red*) loops around the Earth, though its height and angle can vary. A suborbital path (*blue*) is a lower, up-and-down flight.

↑ Neil Armstrong in the cockpit of an X-15 rocket plane. This picture was taken in 1961, eight years before he landed on the Moon with Buzz Aldrin.

??? Did astronauts fly spacecraft with wings?

The X-15 was a rocket plane that could fly very fast and high. Some flights reached more than 50 miles (80 km) high. The U.S. Air Force considers this height to be the **edge of space**. Several X-15 pilots were given an astronaut's badge for these flights. One of these pilots was Neil Armstrong, later to became famous as the first human on the Moon.

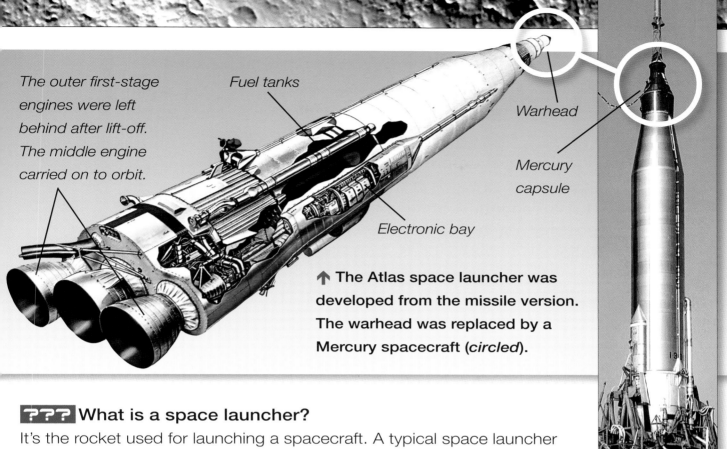

The outer first-stage engines were left behind after lift-off. The middle engine carried on to orbit.

Fuel tanks

Warhead

Mercury capsule

Electronic bay

⬆ The Atlas space launcher was developed from the missile version. The warhead was replaced by a Mercury spacecraft (*circled*).

??? What is a space launcher?

It's the rocket used for launching a spacecraft. A typical space launcher has one or more **stages**, each with its own fuel tanks and rocket motors. Each stage is left behind as its fuel is used up, the next stage taking over to gain more speed and height. Early space launchers were often developed from military missiles. These included the SM-65 Atlas (*above*) of 1959. It was converted to carry the Mercury spacecraft.

> "You've done it in the simulator so many times, you don't have a real sense of being excited when the flight is going on...as soon as the lift-off occurs, you are busy doing what you have to do."
>
> *Alan Shepard, first American in space*

??? What if a launcher exploded?

Early rockets were unreliable, so safety was a key design feature. The LES (Launch Escape System) was developed for the one-seat Mercury capsule. In a takeoff emergency, the LES (*right*) could quickly haul the capsule to safety.

THE FIRST ASTRONAUTS

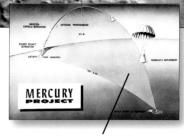

Suborbital flight path of Mercury capsule

In 1961, humans finally left the bonds of Earth. Soviet cosmonaut Yuri Gagarin was the first. He was soon followed by Americans Alan Shepard and John Glenn.

??? When did Yuri Gagarin make his orbital flight?

The first human in space was launched on April 12, 1961, from the Baikonur Cosmodrome in central Asia. Gagarin flew just one orbit of Earth, in a flight that lasted 1 hour and 48 minutes. His flight was celebrated all across the Soviet Union, a group of countries that had been in competition with the United States since the Soviets launched Sputnik 1 in 1957.

↑ Yuri Gagarin flew inside a ball-shaped metal space capsule called the Vostok 3KA.

??? Is there a difference between astronauts and cosmonauts?

Americans decided to use the word astronaut, while the Soviet Union called them cosmonauts. However, both translate similarly as star sailor or space sailor. Other countries have their own labels too, such as the Chinese taikonaut and the French spationaut.

??? Who were the Mercury Seven?

They were the first group of American astronauts (*see page 28*), named after the single-seat Mercury spacecraft that was developed while they were being trained for flight.

The first American in space was Alan Shepard, who flew a suborbital flight a few weeks after Gagarin, on May 5, 1961. And on February 20, 1962, John Glenn flew three orbits in a Mercury spacecraft. These two flights went into the history books.

↑ Three of the Mercury Seven astronauts. From left, Gus Grissom, John Glenn, Alan Shepard.

Orange over-suit, worn to be easily spotted after landing

"Anyone who has spent any time in space will love it for the rest of their lives.
I achieved my childhood dream of the sky."
Valentina Tereshkova, who wanted to fly again in space, but never had another mission

➜ In 1963, the cosmonaut Valentina Tereshkova became the first female in space. Her solo flight in Vostok 6 lasted for 48 orbits.

SCHOOL FOR SPACE

The early years of space flight were full of unknowns. Astronauts were put through difficult tests and simulations.

↑ This centrifuge has a seat inside for the astronaut.

??? What is a centrifuge?

It's a spinning device (*above*) which gives trainee astronauts some of the sensations of flight, especially the massive surge of acceleration felt during takeoff. Normally humans live in Earth's **gravity** (1G), but the thrust of full rocket power can multiply the effect by a chest-crushing four or five times. The centrifuge helped astronauts train for the strain.

← Astronaut David Scott learns about reduced gravity in a "vomit comet" KC-135. Scott flew on the Gemini 8 mission, and went to the Moon on Apollo 15.

"Ever since I was five years old, all I ever wanted to be was a pilot. And flying to the Moon seemed to be the ultimate adventure."
David Scott

??? What was the "vomit comet"?

It's the nickname for a KC-135 jet used for "reduced gravity" training. The jet flies in a special arcing flight called a parabola. Everything inside, including a trainee astronaut, becomes near-weightless for 30 to 40 seconds before the jet levels out and weight returns to normal. Some people feel ill during such a flight, which is why the jet got its nickname!

→ In this ground test, a Gemini spacecraft closes in to dock with an Agena target rocket. The crew is learning the maneuver, ready to try it for real in Earth orbit.

??? Why did Gemini astronauts practice docking maneuvers?

The two-seat Gemini spacecraft came after the smaller Mercury capsule. Gemini allowed astronauts to perfect space maneuvers, so they would be ready for later Apollo Moon landings. As planned, spacecraft dockings were an essential part of the Apollo system.

??? What was a splashdown?

This was how American astronauts returned to Earth. They came down in the Command **Module**, with parachutes slowing their splashdown in the ocean. Helicopters from a recovery ship were soon on the scene to lift them on board.

← Astronauts practice how to leave a Gemini capsule in case it sinks before recovery.

INSIDE MISSION CONTROL

Every space flight is a team effort, in which astronauts and ground teams work together for success.

↑ Ground antennas kept Mission Control in contact with spacecraft.

← Ground stations were marked by circles on the large rear wall screen.

??? What is the job of a CAPCOM?

The term is short for capsule communicator, the person on the ground who links Mission Control with a spacecraft. In the days of Project Mercury, the CAPCOM could have been an astronaut such as Alan Shepard, seen above in front of a TV screen showing another Mercury mission just before takeoff.

Shepard is shown here in the Manned Spacecraft Center in Florida, which was linked to communications antennas around the world. These were placed under the spacecraft flight path, so it passed over each in turn.

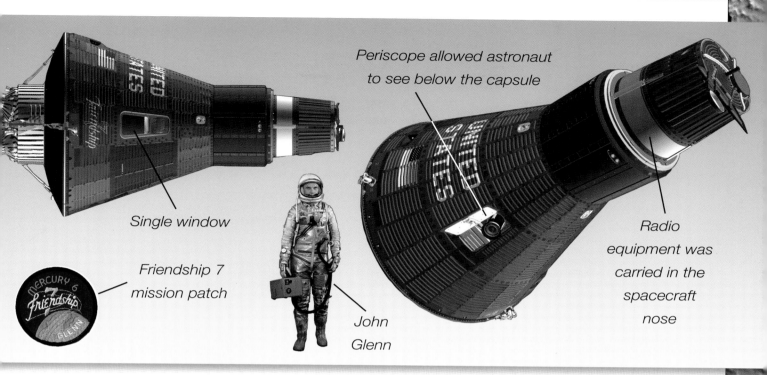

Periscope allowed astronaut to see below the capsule

Single window

Friendship 7 mission patch

John Glenn

Radio equipment was carried in the spacecraft nose

⬆ The Mercury was small, as shown in comparison to John Glenn, who was 5 feet 10 inches (178 cm) tall.

❓❓❓ How did a Mercury astronaut talk to CAPCOM?

John Glenn's Friendship 7 Mercury capsule was equipped with several radio antennas, all packed into the nose compartment.

One huge advantage of a two-way CAPCOM link was that a problem could be discussed immediately. Engineers and scientists on the ground could then come up with a fix for the issue.

"I suppose the one quality in an astronaut more powerful than any other is curiosity. They have to get some place nobody's ever been."
John Glenn, first U.S. astronaut in orbit

Antenna used to communicate with Mission Control

❓❓❓ What about ocean communications?

Recovery ships were part of the worldwide space system, and had antennas to keep Mission Control informed of progress. The USS *Wasp* (*right*) was the ship that recovered the Gemini 6A and 7 spacecraft after their successful splashdown in the Atlantic Ocean.

➜ Gemini 6A and 7 aboard the USS *Wasp*.

IN THE COCKPIT
FLYING A SPACECRAFT

The first astronauts insisted on being able to fly their spacecraft, rather than relying on automatic equipment for total control of a mission.

??? Why were astronauts called "Spam in a can"?
Spam was a type of canned meat, which is how astronauts saw themselves if their flight was automatically controlled. They were aviators, so they believed it was vital to be able to use their flying skills in space.

↑ Pete Conrad (*left*) and Gordon Cooper in the cockpit of Gemini 5, August 1965.

??? Was flight control needed?
Yes, especially as early spacecraft were not very reliable. John Glenn flew his Mercury capsule on manual control for two of three orbits, because the automatic systems had failed. On reentry, he switched to the auxillary system which stabilized the craft.

"It's a magical feeling to climb toward the heavens... You have left that world beneath you. You are inside the sky."
Gordon Cooper

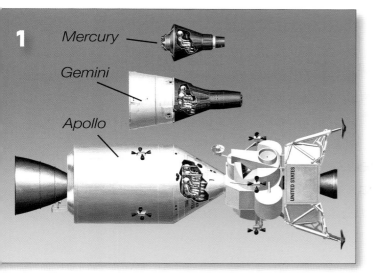

1

Mercury

Gemini

Apollo

UNITED STATES

2

UNITED STATES

Friendship 7

⬆️⬇️ Three spacecraft compared to scale (*1*). John Glenn eases into the Mercury hatch (*2*). The Gemini instrument panel (*3*), and looking inside the Apollo 9 Command Module (*4*).

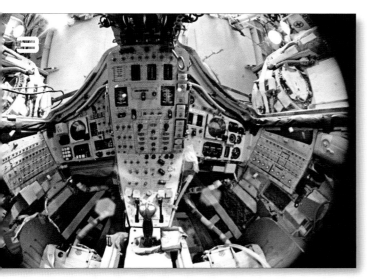

3

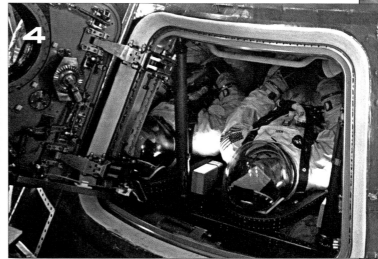

4

❓❓❓ Were different spacecraft similar to fly in?

The basic controls on the Mercury, Gemini, and Apollo were similar, and they all relied on Mission Control for guidance and instructions. Apollo had more room, especially for the one crew member who remained in the capsule while the other two landed on the Moon.

➡️ Apollo modules were connected hatch-to-hatch at various times during each flight.

FOOD AND DRINK
AT HOME IN SPACE

As space missions became longer, astronauts needed to eat and drink in space. This meant new ways of preparing and eating food.

??? What do astronauts drink and eat in space?

In the early days, liquids were limited to water and juice. John Glenn enjoyed an orange drink called Tang.

Food was often freeze-dried, or came ready-to-eat, squeezed out of toothpaste-like tubes (*below*). Bite-sized bread cubes were developed to avoid crumbs floating around the cabin and clogging delicate electronics.

Mercury astronaut sucks food from a plastic pouch

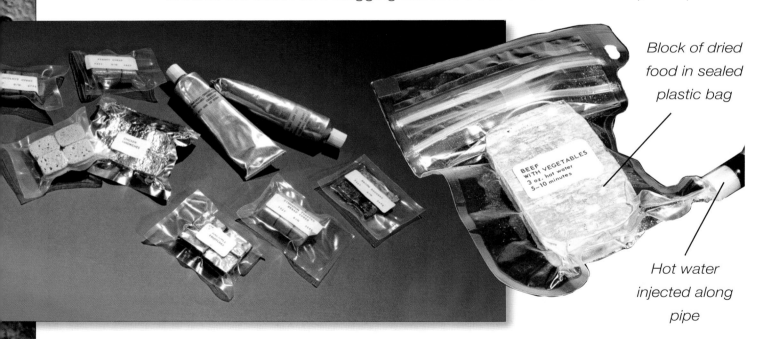

Block of dried food in sealed plastic bag

BEEF VEGETABLES
WITH water
3 oz. hot water
5–10 minutes

Hot water injected along pipe

??? Did astronauts have their own menus?

Food technology improved along with rocket hardware. On Apollo flights, astronauts had menus chosen according to their own tastes, which could include spaghetti and meat sauce, followed by banana and chocolate pudding.

The Apollo Command Module had a hot water supply, so for the first time, space foods could be served piping hot.

↑ **Meals came with simple instructions. Food was mixed with hot water, and could be eaten after a few minutes.**

??? What happened to body waste?

Spacecraft of the 1960s didn't have washrooms, so astronauts had to make do with plastic bags for liquid and solid waste. The material inside was stored and brought back to Earth, even on Apollo missions that lasted for a week or more.

Mercury astronaut Alan Shepard had no storage bag at all on his 1961 flight. The flight was expected to last for about 15 minutes, but very long technical delays before launch forced Shepard to relieve himself directly into his suit!

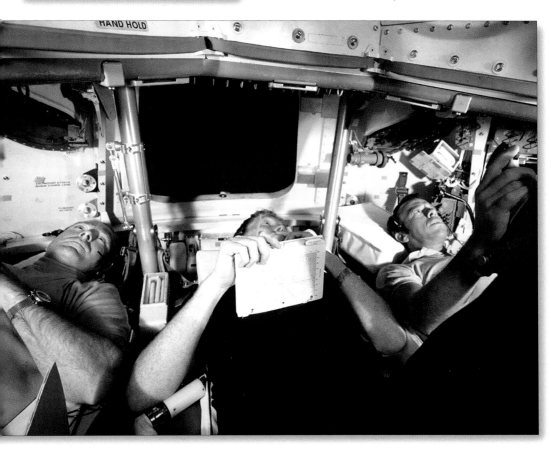

← The crew of Apollo 14 carry out checks in the Command Module simulator before their flight. The real module was exactly the same size, a cramped place that would be their home for a Moon mission lasting nine days.

??? Why was a space pen invented?

Astronauts originally made notes using pencils. But the Fisher Pen Company created the AG-7, a pen (*right*) that could be used upside down, underwater, in hot or cold conditions, and in zero gravity. In 1963, after much testing, NASA ordered 400 Fisher pens for Apollo missions. A year later, the Soviet Union bought 100 of the pens, to be used on future Soyuz flights.

SPACE SUITS

The space suit is an astronaut's essential survival gear. It not only keeps the wearer alive, but also allows for easier movement of their arms and legs.

??? Why is a space suit needed?

In a sealed spacecraft, astronauts can dress in lightweight outfits. But when carrying out any form of extravehicular activity (**EVA**), wearing a space suit is essential. Gemini missions practiced for future Moon flights, which would need EVAs in space. Astronauts also trained for walking on the lunar surface.

→ This suit was worn by Ed White for his Gemini 4 spacewalk.

← Ed White makes the first EVA from a U.S. spacecraft.

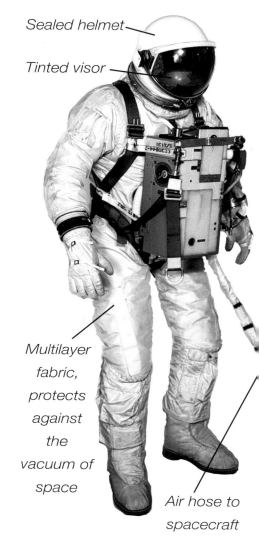

Sealed helmet

Tinted visor

Multilayer fabric, protects against the vacuum of space

Air hose to spacecraft

??? What are the biggest problems with designing a space suit?

A basic issue is that when you pump a suit full of air, it behaves much like a balloon. This makes bending arms and legs difficult, so the limbs need special joints to allow for more freedom of motion.

Controlling humidity in a suit is also important. When an astronaut breathes, they exhale moisture and cannot see out of a fogged-up helmet visor.

"We just kept putting off the worry as we focused on the next problem and how to solve it."

Fred Haise (left) talking about his near-disastrous Apollo 13 mission. He is seen here, training for that flight.

↑ Simulators let astronauts practice walking in the Moon's low gravity.

??? Who first walked in space?

The cosmonaut Alexei Leonov spent several minutes outside the Voskhod 2 spacecraft in March 1965. His suit ballooned out with air pressure and he only just made it safely back inside. The Gemini astronaut Ed White made the first U.S. spacewalk in June 1965.

→ This early space-suit design was a fairly accurate idea of how real suits would look.

WORKING IN SPACE

The first astronauts explored a new environment. No one knew if they could survive at all, let alone stay fit enough to carry out any work.

??? Was there concern for health?

On Earth, astronauts trained in space-like environments so they could discover the effects of space on their bodies. They needed to know if being weightless for hours or days at a time would be harmful. Once in space, they used medication to help them cope with space sickness. This is a condition that causes nausea and dizziness while adjusting to weightlessness.

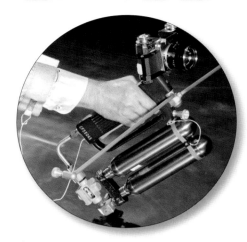

↑ This handheld "gas gun" helped Ed White move around in space.

← Astronaut Ed White leaves the cockpit of Gemini 4 to make the first U.S. spacewalk. He had no problems with the experience, enjoying it so much that he had to be ordered to come back inside!

"Landing on the Moon was a dream that millions of kids have had for hundreds of years."
Russell Schweickart, who took this photo above Earth in March 1969. He was looking across at David Scott from the ladder of the Lunar Module.

??? **Why did Apollo astronauts carry out EVAs?**
Extravehicular activity (EVA) was first called a "spacewalk" by the news media. The Moon-landing program included several EVAs, from walking on the Moon to recovering film canisters from the Apollo Service Module while in space.

↑ David Scott stands up by Apollo 9's open hatch. The crew tested all the Apollo systems to get ready for future Moon landings.

← The Lunar Module Spider was flight tested high in Earth orbit.

??? **What other work did they do?**
The Apollo 9 mission flew in Earth orbit, but tested all parts of the Moon-landing system, including suits as well as spacecraft.

The Lunar Module Spider was flown nearly 111 miles (180 km) away from the Command Module, named Gumdrop.

FOOTSTEPS ON THE MOON

The Mercury, Gemini, and Apollo flights ultimately led to success. Six out of seven Apollo missions landed safely on the Moon, allowing a dozen astronauts to explore the dusty orb.

??? Were the space suits used on the Moon reliable?

They were first tested by Neil Armstrong and Buzz Aldrin of Apollo 11, after their Moon landing of July 20, 1969. Neil and Buzz spent just over two hours in their suits, walking on the Moon. But the last Apollo 17 mission lasted about three days—all without a serious technical hitch from the space suits.

← Leaving the Lunar Module's porch and going up or down the ladder demanded good balance from the astronauts.

??? Were the bulky space suits difficult to walk in?

Apollo astronauts practiced on Earth long before their flights took off. This training gave them a good idea of what they would experience on the Moon.

The low lunar gravity was a great help, and astronauts found no real problems after they landed.

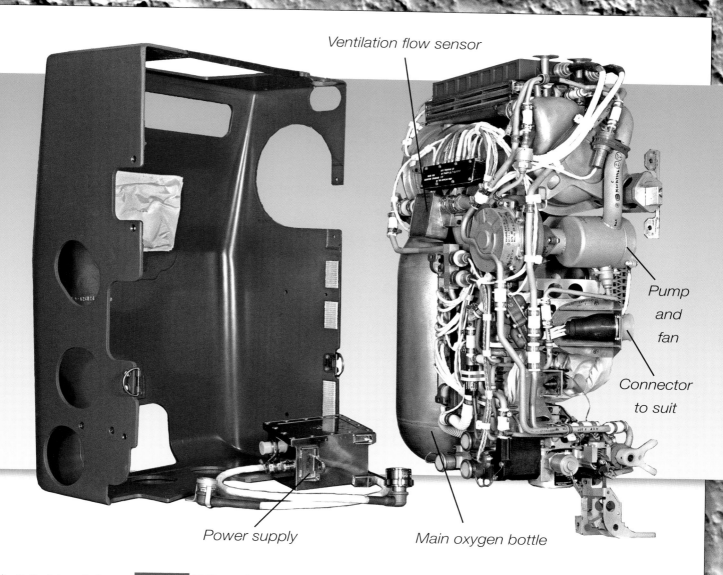

Ventilation flow sensor

Pump
and
fan

Connector
to suit

Power supply

Main oxygen bottle

⬆ A lightweight cover slipped over the PLSS when worn on the back of a space suit.

??? What is a PLSS?

The Portable Life Support System (PLSS) was devised to allow an astronaut to leave a spacecraft safely. The PLSS is a complex piece of gear that regulates a suit's air pressure, supplies breathable air, removes waste gases, and keeps humidity under control.

"Up there, I weighed only 50 pounds (22 kg). So I could prance around on my toes. It was quite easy to do."
Alan Bean, talking about walking in the Moon's low gravity during his Apollo 12 mission of November 1969

➔ Neil Armstrong's Apollo 11 space suit, laid out after his return to Earth.

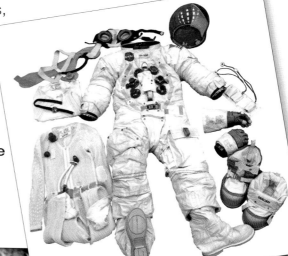

PRESSURE SUIT TO MOON SUIT

The design of space suits showed steady progress. By 1969, Moon suits allowed astronauts to explore safely for hours at a time.

An early high-altitude flight suit

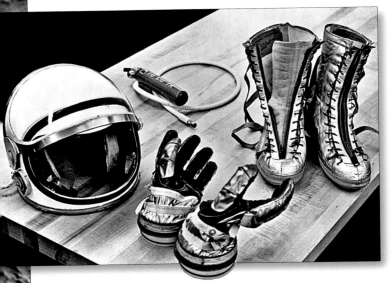

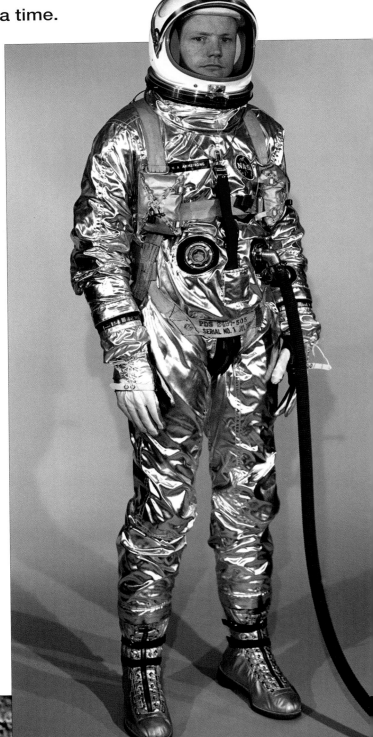

??? Were Mercury suits specially made?

Yes, but they were based on pressure suits already in use by high-flying jet pilots. Mercury astronauts each had three suits. One suit was used for training, another was used for the flight, and a third suit was needed in case there were problems with the flight suit. The suits were reliable, so the third often wasn't used.

↑ **Checked and ready-to-wear suit items laid out for a Mercury mission.**

→ Neil Armstrong in an early Gemini G2C suit, worn during training. The long hose is for his air supply.

??? Were space suits comfortable to wear?

Improving comfort was a key aim, though the Gemini suit was based on an existing item worn by X-15 pilots.

The Gemini suit was made of multiple layers of nylon, and a fire-resistant fabric called Nomex. It suited the two-seat Gemini cockpit, but Apollo flights would last for a week or more. A better solution was to reserve space suits for EVAs, and wear lightweight coveralls at other times.

↑ The blue chest pack on this Gemini suit is the emergency life-support system.

→ Apollo suit with PLSS, seen here during the Apollo 17 mission of 1972.

??? What extras did an Apollo Moon suit have?

The main extra was the PLSS, which provided life support the entire time an astronaut was outside the Lunar Module. It looks extremely bulky, but astronauts had few problems during spacewalks. Alan Shepard was even able swing a golf club!

NEAR SIDE AND FAR SIDE

Astronauts on Apollo missions helped map the Moon closely. And they passed over the far side, which we cannot see from the Earth.

Earth

Moon

↑ Earth and the Moon, shown to the same scale.

??? Why does the Moon have two sides?

The Moon's familiar face remains the same because our natural **satellite** rotates in the same time that it completes an orbit around Earth, about every 29.5 days.

No one knew what the far side looked like until the first space probes took photos in the 1960s. The Apollo 8 mission of 1968 marked the first time that humans saw it.

↓ The Moon's near side (*left*) and far side. Apollo 11 passed over the crater Daedalus (*arrowed*).

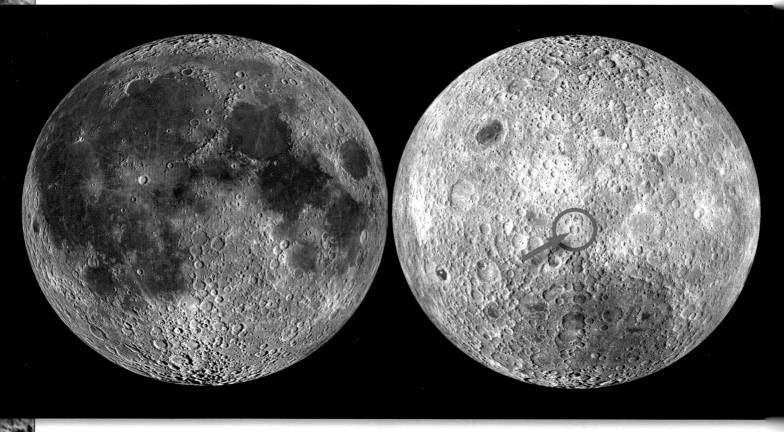

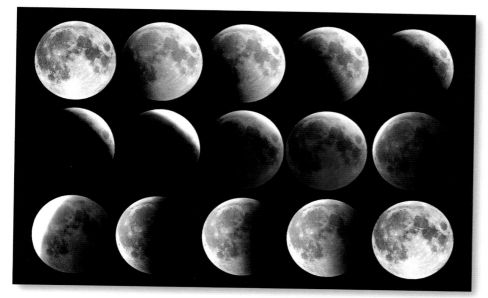

??? How long does a lunar day last?

Because the Moon rotates once every 29.5 Earth days, a lunar day and night each lasts just over two weeks.

The temperature in direct sunlight can reach up to 253 °Fahrenheit (123 °C), but in the shadows it can fall to −280 °Fahrenheit (−170 °C).

↑ A sequence of photos taken over a lunar month. The Moon sometimes passes into the Earth's shadow, when it looks a coppery-red shade.

??? Has an astronaut walked on the far side?

No—all the Apollo missions landed on the near side, where it was easier to remain in communication with the astronauts. An early space probe crashed on the far side, and in 2019, China safely landed a lunar rover there.

← Apollo astronauts took many photos of the Moon, including crater Daedalus on the far side (*opposite*).

"It really makes you wonder about our place in the Universe and what we're all about. When you see that many stars out there you realize that those are really suns, and those suns could have planets around them..."
Al Worden, Apollo 15

TIMELINE

A look at the astronauts and cosmonauts featured in this book. They are among the space pioneers who helped to blaze a trail from Earth to the Moon.

Edwin "Buzz" Aldrin (1930–)
Lunar Module pilot of Apollo 11, and second human to walk on the Moon. A former U.S. Air Force pilot, he also flew on Gemini 12.

Neil Armstrong (1930–2012)
Lunar Module commander of Apollo 11, he was the first human on the Moon. A naval aviator and test pilot, he also flew the X-15 rocket plane, and Gemini 8 with David Scott.

Alan Bean (1932–2018)
Lunar Module pilot of Apollo 12.

A former naval aviator and test pilot, he later became an artist whose work often depicted the Moon.

Charles "Pete" Conrad (1930–1999)
Flew on Gemini 5 and 11, and was the third human on the Moon during the Apollo 12 mission.

Gordon "Gordo" Cooper (1927–2004)
A former U.S. Air Force test pilot, he flew on Mercury and Gemini missions, achieving a total of 222 hours in space.

Yuri Gagarin (1934–1968)
Soviet pilot and cosmonaut. He became the first human in space in 1961, completing one orbit around Earth.

← The Mercury Seven astronauts selected for Project Mercury. Back row from left: Alan Shepard, Gus Grissom, Gordon Cooper. Front row: Wally Schirra, Deke Slayton, John Glenn, Scott Carpenter.

John Glenn (1921–2016)
A former U.S. Marine Corps pilot, he was the first American in orbit, circling Earth three times in 1962.

Virgil "Gus" Grissom (1926–1967)
Pilot of Liberty Bell 7, the second Mercury suborbital flight in 1961. He also flew on Gemini 3, but died in 1967 when the Command Module of Apollo 1 caught fire.

Fred Haise (1933–)
He was the Lunar Module pilot of Apollo 13, but an oxygen tank exploded on the way to the Moon and the crew was lucky to return to Earth alive.

Alexei Leonov (1934–)
A Soviet cosmonaut, he made the world's first space walk, from Voskhod 2 in 1965. He made colored sketches while in space, and continued this work in retirement.

David "Dave" Scott (1932–)
First flew in space on Gemini 8, later flew on Apollo 9 in Earth orbit. Commander of Apollo 15, he was the first person to drive on the Moon in the LRV (Lunar Roving Vehicle).

Russell "Rusty" Schweickart (1935–)
Flew on the 1969 Apollo 9 mission. Tested the Apollo suit, including the PLSS.

Alan Shepard (1923–1998)
First American to fly into space in 1961. Ten years later, he landed on the Moon with the Apollo 14 mission.

↑ A life-size Mercury spacecraft model is shown here being tested in a wind tunnel. Such a machine helps to show whether the spacecraft will be stable in flight.

Valentina Tereshkova (1937–)
Soviet cosmonaut who became the first woman in space in 1963. Her flight lasted nearly three days.

Edward "Ed" White (1930–1967)
Made the first American space walk from Gemini 4 in 1965. He died in the Apollo 1 fire of 1967.

"There were more stars in the sky than I had expected. The sky was deep black, yet at the same time bright with sunlight."
Alexei Leonov, on the view outside his spacecraft window

GLOSSARY

Apollo The U.S. Moon-landing program, named after the Greek and Roman god of light and beauty

centrifuge Machine that rotates. In space training it simulates increased forces felt by astronauts, especially during takeoff, reentry, and landing.

docking Procedure in which two spacecraft approach each other, then link together

edge of space Space has no real edge, as the atmosphere just gets thinner as you gain height. However, at 62 miles (100 km) high, there is little or no air, and this is known as the Karman line. Alan Shepard's Mercury flight of 1961 reached 116 miles (187 km).

EVA Short for extravehicular activity, another term for a space walk

gravity The force of attraction between objects. The Moon has six times less gravity than Earth, so a 132-pound (60 kg) weight on Earth weighs just 22 pounds (10 kg) on the Moon. In orbit, objects (including astronauts) experience zero gravity (zero-g), or weightlessness.

module Section of a spacecraft that links with another. The Apollo system consisted of a number of such modules:

    CM Command Module

    SM Service Module

    LM Lunar Module

NASA National Air and Space Administration, the U.S. space agency

orbit The curving path that one space object takes around another

pressure suit Suit that protects the wearer from lack of air at high altitudes

← Mercury astronauts train aboard a vomit comet aircraft, used to provide short periods of reduced gravity.

⬆ Alan Shepard being winched aboard a recovery helicopter in 1961. He had just splashed down in the Freedom 7 Mercury spacecraft (*arrowed*).

reentry Term for returning to Earth through the atmosphere

satellite A space object that orbits a bigger one. The Moon is Earth's natural satellite, while any orbiting spacecraft is an artificial satellite until it leaves orbit.

Soviet Union A group of 15 states, including Russia, that existed from 1922 to 1991. In the 1960s, the Soviet Union competed with the U.S. to try to win the Space Race to the Moon.

splashdown Final part of a Mercury, Gemini, or Apollo mission, when the reentry module landed in the sea under large parachutes

Sputnik Word used for several early Soviet satellites. It means "fellow traveler."

stage Part of a rocket, usually one of several used to boost a rocket into space. Typically ejected and left behind when empty of fuel. The descent stage of the Apollo Lunar Module acted as a landing platform, then it became a takeoff pad for the ascent stage.

WEBFINDER

There is plenty of Internet information on astronauts, and even more on the Moon and space exploration. Try these sites to start with, then you can carry on to make your own online explorations.

www.buzzaldrin.com
Buzz Aldrin has an interesting personal website, full of news, events, and videos to watch.

www.canada.ca/en/space-agency
Canada's space industry has a long history, and its present-day robotic equipment works hard in orbit. Start here to find the whole story.

www.esa.int
The main site for the European Space Agency, which has projects ranging from astronauts in orbit to exploring other planets.

www.nasa.gov
The gold standard for space research, including Mercury, Gemini, Apollo, and other programs. Just use the search box to find out more.

Is space flight all a hoax?
It's a question that's asked from time to time, especially by people who don't believe the Apollo Moon flights really happened. The lunar landing was televised live in 1969. Astronauts took many photos of space and the Moon. They also left equipment on the Moon that scientists on Earth used to conduct experiments. If the landing was not real, the experiments would not have been possible.

INDEX

ABOUT THE AUTHOR

David Jefferis has written many information books on science and technology.

His works include a seminal series called World of the Future, as well as more than 40 science books for Crabtree Publishing.

David's merits include winning the London Times Educational Supplement Award, and also Best Science Books of the Year.

At the time of the Apollo landings, he created news graphics for the international media, and has been a keen enthusiast for space flight and high tech ever since.

Follow David online at:
www.davidjefferis.com